William John Macquorn Rankine

Songs and Fables

Illus. by F.B

William John Macquorn Rankine

Songs and Fables
Illus. by F.B

ISBN/EAN: 9783744767378

Printed in Europe, USA, Canada, Australia, Japan

Cover: Foto ©Andreas Hilbeck / pixelio.de

More available books at **www.hansebooks.com**

SONGS AND FABLES.

PUBLISHED BY

JAMES MACLEHOSE, GLASGOW.

MACMILLAN AND CO., LONDON.

London,	. .	*Hamilton, Adams and Co.*
Cambridge,	.	*Macmillan and Co.*
Edinburgh,	.	*Edmonston and Douglas.*
Dublin,	. .	*W. H. Smith and Sons*

MDCCCLXXIV.

SONGS AND FABLES

BY

WILLIAM J. MACQUORN RANKINE

LATE PROFESSOR OF CIVIL ENGINEERING AND MECHANICS IN THE
UNIVERSITY OF GLASGOW

WITH ILLUSTRATIONS BY J. B.

GLASGOW: JAMES MACLEHOSE
PUBLISHER TO THE UNIVERSITY

LONDON: MACMILLAN AND CO.
1874

THOSE who enjoyed the personal intimacy of the late Professor Rankine—and the circle was not a narrow one—will, it is thought, be glad to have the means of recalling some of the songs which they can no longer hear from him, though his voice and manner lent a charm which the printed page cannot restore.

Those who knew him from his graver works only, may be surprised, but it is hoped will not be disappointed, to find that a genius for philosophic research, which made his name known throughout the whole scientific world—and the labours of a life devoted chiefly to directing others, from the chair, and by the press, how to follow his steps—were not incompatible with the playful, genial spirit which brightens the following pages.

The first of the Songs may be taken as the meeting-point of science and humour:—the last possesses a melancholy interest, from having been written very shortly before his death, when failing health and eye-sight seem to have revived a longing for the scenery and simple pleasures of his childhood.

Three of the Songs have already been published in *Blackwood's Magazine*, whose proprietors have kindly consented to their re-appearing in the present volume. One or two have been issued separately, along with their airs and accompaniments·; and some others will probably be published in that form, for the use of those to whom the music is an essential or principal attraction.

The Fables explain, in a mode not attempted by archæologists, the origin and meaning of some of our old and popular sign-boards. The illustrations attached to them, from the well known pencil of a gifted lady connected with the same University, will serve to enliven a humour which some readers might consider dry.

May, 1874.

CONTENTS.

𝔖ongs.

Fables.

CONTENTS.

LIST OF ILLUSTRATIONS.

Songs.

A

MATHEMATICIAN IN LOVE.

I.

A MATHEMATICIAN fell madly in love
   With a lady, young, handsome, and charming:
By angles and ratios harmonic he strove
Her curves and proportions all faultless to prove,
   As he scrawled hieroglyphics alarming.

II.

He measured with care, from the ends of a base,
   The arcs which her features subtended:
Then he framed transcendental equations, to trace
The flowing outlines of her figure and face,
   And thought the result very splendid.

III.

He studied (since music has charms for the fair)
  The theory of fiddles and whistles,—
Then composed, by acoustic equations, an air,
Which, when 'twas performed, made the lady's long hair
  Stand on end, like a porcupine's bristles.

IV.

The lady loved dancing:—he therefore applied,
  To the polka and waltz, an equation ;
But when to rotate on his axis he tried,
His centre of gravity swayed to one side,
  And he fell, by the earth's gravitation.

V.

No doubts of the fate of his suit made him pause,
  For he proved, to his own satisfaction,
That the fair one returned his affection;—"because,
" As every one knows, by mechanical laws,
  " Re-action is equal to action."

VI.

"Let x denote beauty,—y, manners well-bred,—
 "z, Fortune,—(this last is essential),—
"Let L stand for love"—our philosopher said,—
"Then L is a function of x, y, and z,
 "Of the kind which is known as potential."

VII.

"Now integrate L with respect to $d\,t$,
 "(t Standing for time and persuasion);
"Then, between proper limits, 'tis easy to see,
"The definite integral *Marriage* must be :—
 "(A very concise demonstration)."

VIII.

Said he—"If the wandering course of the moon
 "By Algebra can be predicted,
"The female affections must yield to it soon"—
—But the lady ran off with a dashing dragoon,
 And left him amazed and afflicted.

Equation referred to in Stanza VI.—

$$L = \phi(x, y, z)$$

$$= \iiint \frac{f(x, y, z)}{\sqrt{(\xi - x)^2 + (\eta - y)^2 + (\zeta - z)^2}} \, d\xi \, d\eta \, d\zeta.$$

Equation referred to in Stanza VII.—

$$\int_{-\infty}^{+\infty} L \, dt = M$$

COACHMAN OF THE "SKYLARK."

Air—" Four high-mettled steeds."

In the good old times, before railways were known, the "Skylark," on the —— and —— road, was the fastest coach, and its driver, Joseph ——, the best and smartest coachman in England. The "Skylark" has long ago gone the way of all coaches ; and Joe is now landlord of the "Horns," at ——, where long may he flourish !

I.

YE passengers so bothered,
Who snore in rattling trains,
By dusty vapour smothered,
Awake, and hear my strains !
I 'll tell you of the good old days,
For ever past and gone,

Before your pestilent railways
  Had spoiled all sorts of fun,—
When Joe, with light but steady hand,
Did four high-mettled steeds command,
And well was known, through all the land,
  The Coachman of the "Skylark."

II.

Can any greasy stoker
  With dashing Joe compare?
He was a jovial joker,
  And company most rare.
Then wind and weather we defied,
  We scorned your well glazed car,
And gladly on the box would ride,
  To smoke a mild cigar
With Joe, whose light but steady hand
Did four high-mettled steeds command;—
Oh! well was known, through all the land,
  The Coachman of the "Skylark."

III.

Where your long, dismal tunnel
    Gropes through yon lofty hill
(A pitch-dark, noisome funnel,
    That might Old Harry kill),
We, on the "Skylark," used to glide
    Up from the smiling vale,
And on the mountain's heathy side
    The freshening breeze inhale,
While Joe, with light but steady hand,
Did four high-mettled steeds command ;—
Oh! well was known, through all the land,
    The Coachman of the "Skylark."

IV.

Where yon embankment ugly
    Has marred the pleasant scene,
A little inn stood snugly
    Beside the village green :
'Twas there the "Skylark" stopped to dine,
    And famous was the cheer ;

Good were the victuals, old the wine,
And strong the foaming beer
For Joe, whose light but steady hand
Did four high-mettled steeds command ;—
Oh ! well was known, through all the land,
The Coachman of the " Skylark."

V.

And one dwelt in that valley
Would make a desert shine :
The sparkling eyes of Sally
Eclipsed her father's wine.
Oh ! where 's the flinty heart that could
Withstand that lovely lass,
As smiling at the bar she stood,
And filled a parting glass
For Joe, whose light but steady hand
Did four high-mettled steeds command ;—
Oh ! well was known, through all the land,
The Coachman of the " Skylark."

VI.

Those days are gone for ever—
   The "Skylark" is no more;
And poor old Joe shall never
   More drive his coach-and-four.
Then let us to the "Horns" repair,
   And, with a flowing bowl,
Let's strive to banish grief and care,
   And cheer the good old soul
Of Joe, whose light but steady hand
Did once four mettled steeds command,
When well was known, through all the land,
   The Coachman of the "Skylark!"

1844.

ENGINE-DRIVER TO HIS ENGINE.

Air—"The Iron Horse."

I.

PUT forth your force, my iron horse, with limbs
  that never tire !
The best of oil shall feed your joints, and the best
  ' of coal your fire ;
So off we tear from Euston Square, to beat the
  swift south wind,
As we rattle along the North-West rail, with the
  express train behind :—
  Dash along, crash along, sixty miles an hour !
  Right through old England flee !
  For I am bound to see my love,
  Far away in the North Countrie.

II.

Like a train of ghosts, the telegraph posts go wildly
trooping by,
While one by one the milestones run, and off
behind us fly :
Like foaming wine it fires my blood to see your
lightning speed,—
Arabia's race ne'er matched your pace, my gallant
steam-borne steed !
Wheel along, squeal along, sixty miles an hour !
Right through old England flee !
For I am bound to see my love,
Far away in the North Countrie.

III.

My blessing on old George Stephenson ! let his
fame for ever last ;
For he was the man that found the plan to make
you run so fast :
His arm was strong, his head was long, he knew
not guile nor fear ;

When I think of him, it makes me proud that *I*
    am an engineer!
  Tear along, flare along, sixty miles an hour!
  Right through old England flee!
  For I am bound to see my love,
    Far away in the North Countrie.

IV.

Now Thames and Trent are far behind, and evening's
    shades are come;
Before my eyes the brown hills rise that guard my
    true love's home:
Even now she stands, my own dear lass! beside the
    cottage door,
And she listens for the whistle shrill, and the blast-
    pipe's rattling roar:—
  Roll along, bowl along, sixty miles an hour!
  Right through old England flee!
  For I am bound to see my love,
    At home in the North Countrie.

1859.

IR O N.

A Geological, Economical, and Patriotic Song.

I.

MYRIADS of ages ere this earth
Beheld the first of human birth,
When o'er the future Britain rolled
The monster-teeming Ocean old,
Deep in the bosom of this land
Heaven sowed the seed with bounteous hand,
Whence Britain's strength and glory spring,
IRON, the Metals' mighty king.

II.

We envy not those distant lands
Whose rivers roll o'er golden sands ;
Rich in the nobler metal we,
That guides the ship o'er trackless sea—
That digs the mine—that tills the plain—
That bears and drives the flying train—
That wealth in every shape bestows,
And arms our hands against our foes.

III.

Yet not in lifeless ore alone
Does Britain Iron's virtues own.
Man nor the elements can foil
The children of the Iron soil.
'Tis their's to wield resistless might,
Danger, and toil, and death to slight,
In every clime between the poles,
With Iron frames and Iron souls.

1849.

WHAT SHALL WE DO FOR COAL?

Air—" Ioly goode Ale and olde."

I.

WITH furnace fierce in forge and mill,
  And steamships on the foam,
And trains that sweep through vale and hill,
  And roaring fires at home,
In warmth and wealth while we rejoice,
  Nor heed the risk we run,
Geology, with warning voice,
  Says, "Coal will soon be done :
      Then forge and mill must all stand still,
      And trains no longer roll,
      Nor longer float the swift steamboat ;
      Oh ! what shall we do for Coal?

B

II.

" For countless ages forests dark
　Grew thick o'er Britain's isle ;
For countless ages wood and bark
　Lay deep beneath her soil.
The old black diamond may appear
　As though 'twould ne'er give o'er ;
But seventy million tons a-year
　Will soon exhaust the store :
　　　Then forge and mill must all stand still,
　　　And trains no longer roll,
　　　Nor longer float the swift steamboat ;
　　　Oh ! what shall we do for Coal?

III.

Our goods by horse and cart must go,
　By coach-and-four the mail ;
Our travellers walk, swim, ride, or row,
　And steam give place to sail ;
From wind and water we must try
　To draw what help we can,

While sticks and straw our clothes must dry,
  And boil the pot and pan ;
    And forge and mill must all stand still,
      And trains no longer roll,
      Nor longer float the swift steamboat ;
      Oh ! what shall we do for Coal ?"

IV.

If Britain's hopes on Coal depend,
  Her race is well nigh run ;
Decline and fall her realm attend,
  As soon as Coal is done :
Yet Britain flourished long before
  Her treasures black were found ;
And worth and valour, as of yore,
  'Gainst wealth may hold their ground.
    Though forge and mill should all stand still,
      Cheer up, each valiant soul !
    While Britain can breed British Man,
      We never need care for Coal !

THE THREE-FOOT RULE.

A Song about Standards of Measure.

Air—" The Poacher."

I.

WHEN I was bound apprentice, and learned to use
  my hands,
Folk never talked of measures that came from
  foreign lands :
Now I'm a British Workman, too old to go to
  school ;
So whether the chisel or file I hold, I 'll stick to
  my three-foot rule.

II.

Some talk of millimetres, and some of kilogrammes,
And some of decilitres, to measure beer and drams;
But I'm a British Workman, too old to go to school;
So by pounds I'll eat, and by quarts I'll drink, and
    I'll work by my three-foot rule.

III.

A party of astronomers went measuring of the earth,
And forty million metres they took to be it's girth;
Five hundred million inches, though, go through
    from pole to pole;
So let's stick to inches, feet, and yards, and the
    good old three-foot rule.

IV.

The great Egyptian pyramid's a thousand yards about;
And when the masons finished it, they raised a
    joyful shout;

The chap that planned that building, I'm bound he
   was no fool ;
And now 'tis proved beyond a doubt he used a
   three-foot rule.

V.

Here's a health to every learned man that goes by
   common sense,
And would not plague the workman on any vain
   pretence ;
But as for those philanthropists who'd send us back
   to school,
Oh, *bless* their eyes, if ever they tries to put down
   the three-foot rule !

British Association ; 1864.

DREAMS OF MY YOUTH.

ON RE-VISITING ———.

I.

OH blest were the days when I cared not for
   money,
   When the hours were all sunny that beamed on
      my youth,
When with visions of beauty my fancy was glowing,
   And my heart was o'erflowing with love and with
      truth.

II.

Not lonely, as now, through these woods did I wander,
  Not then did I ponder on fortune's fell strokes,
For I revelled in bliss which I fancied unfading
    As I kissed my sweet maiden beneath the broad
    oaks.

III.

Oh, why fades the passion that once seemed so
    deathless?
  Oh, why is she faithless? and why am I cold?
'Tis the demon of wealth that with envy has seen us,
  And raised up between us a barrier of gold.

IV.

But vain is my sorrow, thus idly bewailing
  The dreams unavailing that memory evokes:
Farewell, then, fair scene of delusion so tender!
  No more shall I wander beneath the broad oaks.

1849.

THE LASS OF URR.

The picturesque and rugged coast of the Stewartry offers remarkable facilities for the contraband trade, which was there carried on with great activity and success up to a comparatively recent period. During the last century, indeed, many families, now opulent and distinguished, were founded by the daring adventurers, enriched by a pursuit which was then, like black-mail and treason, considered a gentlemanly crime.

The Water of Urr, well known for the mingled wildness and beauty of its scenery, was a favourite resort of smugglers. To one of those heroes, known (probably from the locality of his birth) by the name of Rab o' Buittle, the following rude lyric, and the wild and singular air to which it is sung, are ascribed. He appears, like many of his compeers, to have made his fortune by his profession, and settled in life; and, from the allusion to the wigs of the Scottish bar, it may be inferred that he at one time held the respectable position called by poor Peter Peebles "Dominus Litis," and very naturally congratulated himself on escaping therefrom.

I.

FAREWEEL Auld Reekie's stink and stour,
And learned pows weel dredged wi' flour;
Langer here I downa bide,—
Fivescore miles this night I 'll ride !

Up the Tweed and down the Annan,
By Dalskairth and through Kirkgunzeon ;—
Oh ! sweet's the lass will welcome me
Upon the banks of Urr.

II.

'Twas on a night o' driftin' snaw,
And wild the wintry gusts did blaw;
My men and I did hetly spur
Wi' kegs o' brandy up Glen-Urr.
At bein Dalbeattie up I drew
To wat my grey mear's weary mou'.
'Twas then I lost my heart to thee,
My bonny lass of Urr !

III.

"Sweet lass ! an honest heart forgie,
If rough and plain I speak to thee ;
For courtly phrase nae time hae I,
The red-coats follow, we maun fly ;—

Thou art the fairest e'er I saw,
I'll lo'e thee weel while breath I draw;
And soon will I return to thee,
My winsome lass of Urr!"

IV.

E'en sae I spak my mind fu' braid,
Just reived ae kiss, and aff I rade;
Sinsyne I've mony a peril passed,
But now I'm free frae toil at last.
Flee like fire, my guid grey mear,
Till to my breast I brizz my dear!
Oh! blythe, blythe, will our meeting be
Upon the banks of Urr!

I.

WHERE the Midland Sea and the Ocean meet,
  Stands a corner of British ground ;
There the wild waves dash at a mountain's feet,
  With a giant fortress crowned.
The Spaniard casts a jealous eye,
As he sees our flag from the summit fly ;—
For the Dons may come and the Dons may go,
And frown and strut on the shore below ;
But they never shall have Gibraltar—No !
  They never shall have Gibraltar !

II.

'Twas a British fleet, in days of old,
  To the Straits came, westward bound,
When Sir George Rooke, our Admiral bold,
  Resolved on a deed renowned ;—
Says he, "That castle may serve, some day,
To guard old England's blue highway;"
And he swore that the Dons might come or go,
And the Dons might fight, both high and low ;
But they should not keep Gibraltar—No !
  They should not keep Gibraltar !

III.

The brave old Admiral kept his word,
  And the mighty fortress won ;
And what he took by the gun and sword,
  We have kept by the sword and gun.
The last time was, when France and Spain
'Gainst Elliott strove four years in vain ;
For the Dons might come, and the Dons might go,

And bring allies to aid the blow;
But they never could take Gibraltar—No !
  They never could take Gibraltar !

IV.

Oh ! ne'er let us speak of yielding back
  That gem of Britain's crown !
Where our fathers planted the Union Jack,
  Shall their children haul it down?
The strongest fort is justly due
To those who can take it and hold it too :—
So the Dons may come, and the Dons may go,
And frown and strut on the shore below;
But they never shall have Gibraltar—No !
  They never shall have Gibraltar !

THE DASHING YOUNG FELLOW.

Air—" The Charming Woman."

I.

So Pygwyggyne is going to marry—
    What a number of hearts it will vex !
In fact it will quite play old Harry
    With the feelings of half the fair sex.
I believe he's of kin to a Duke,
    Or a Marquis, or else to an Earl ;
And I know he's a dashing young fellow,
    And she's a most fortunate girl !

II.

Yes, indeed, he's a dashing young fellow—·
　　A three-bottle man, as they say ;
And he's always good-natured when mellow,
　　As long as he gets his own way.
Cards, billiards, and hazard he'll play,—
　　His whiskers most charmingly curl—
In short, he's a dashing young fellow,
　　And she's a most fortunate girl !

III.

His horse he can sit like a centaur,
　　He rides like a trump to the hounds ;
His tailor he owes, I may venture
　　To say, ten or twelve hundred pounds.
His bills and his bets have no bounds,
　　He can fence, box, row, steer, reef, and furl—
Oh, by Jove ! he's a dashing young fellow,
　　And she's a most fortunate girl !

IV.

Though to business he never attended,
　His great talents for it appear,—
For he lives in a style that is splendid,
　On an income of—nothing a year.
Now his bride's handsome fortune will clear
　(For the present) his credit from peril—
In fact, he's a dashing young fellow,
　And she's a most fortunate girl !

V.

He keeps dogs and guns in large forces,
　A tiger (a comical elf),
And seven or eight tall Irish horses,
　Which he loves more than aught save himself.
That he marries the lady for pelf
　Sure none can suspect but a churl—
For you know he's a dashing young fellow,
　And she's a most fortunate girl !

VI.

At the pistol to none he 'll surrender,
  As witness his deeds at Chalk Farm ;
Yet his heart as a dove's is as tender,
  For to every fair face it can warm.
I would not the ladies alarm,
  But you know good advice is a pearl—
DON'T MARRY A DASHING YOUNG FELLOW,
  IF YOU ARE A SENSIBLE GIRL !

THE FALLEN TREE.

My Dear L.,

The other evening, whilst walking in Richmond Park alone, as I was approaching the gate leading to the "Star and Garter," I overtook our old friend Theopompus Gubbins, crawling at a snail's pace, and wearing an aspect of the deepest dejection. Wishing for a companion at the dinner which I meditated, I accosted Gubbins, and endeavoured by cheerful conversation to dispel his melancholy. At first my efforts were fruitless; and, although I succeeded in leading him into the "Star and Garter," he for some time pertinaciously refused even the slightest refection.

At length it occurred to me to urge him to disburden his mind of the cause of his despondency. This suggestion he promptly followed, by calling for pen, ink, and paper, and writing the verses of which I annex a copy. The relief given by this effusion was complete. During the exquisite little dinner which followed, Theopompus' spirits continued to rise; and in the evening he evinced even more than his usual convivial talent.

The verses are passable, and might have been better had the author deigned to avail himself of some suggestions of mine for their improvement. I give them as he wrote them, adding my own proposed emendations in the form of Notes.

Believe me,

Ever yours,

R.

London, 1857.

LINES

On revisiting the FALLEN TREE, beside the little old saw-pit, in the wood on the hill in Richmond Park, about half-a-mile S.S.E. of the "Star and Garter." BY THEOPOMPUS GUBBINS. With Notes by a friend of the Author.

Richmond. 1857.

I.

ON a hill in Richmond Park waves a grove perplexed
and dark,
    Where the Cockneys fear to ramble lest they lose
their way,
.Where the foliage hides the sky, and the fern grows
shoulder-high,
    And beneath the oak's broad branches nods the
foxglove gay ;
And a grassy track, made clear through the brake by
roaming deer,
    Winds amidst the deepest shadow of that wild wood
free,
To a lovely place and still, on the summit of the hill,

Where, beside a moss-grown sawpit, lies a fallen
    tree.*

II.

'Twas a day of sunbeams bright—of breezes fresh and
    light—
A foretaste of the summer in the early spring ; †
When first I wandered there, while my maiden sweet
    and fair ‡
Tripped by my side o'er cool green sward and fairy-ring ;
We cheered the forest walk with unconnected talk,
    With goblin tales, and ancient songs, and child-like
      glee ; §

---

* Considering the "saw-pit" to be an unpoetical object, I proposed to Gubbins
to alter the line as follows : " Where, forgotten by the woodman, lies a fallen
tree ; " to which he answered, that the saw-pit really existed, and that he was
resolved to describe the locality exactly.

† Here I reminded Theopompus that, in the "early spring," the foxglove is
not in flower, nor does the fern grow "shoulder-high." His (utterly irrelevant)
reply was, " I 'm not writing a treatise on Botany."

‡ In the author's private copy, which he keeps in the inside breast-pocket of his
coat, I believe that, instead of the word "maiden," there is an abbreviated
female Christian name ; but I could not prevail on Theopompus to divulge it.

§ Here I proposed to Gubbins that he should add some of these "goblin
tales" and "ancient songs" by way of Appendix to his poem ; but he declared
that grief had effaced them all from his memory.

We wreathed our heads with flowers, whence the dew-
  drops shook in showers,
  Till the winding pathway led us to the fallen tree.

III.

As we sat there, side by side, o'er our spirits seemed to
  glide
  A deep and wild emotion that repressed our mirth ;
Then I clasped her to my breast, saying, " Loveliest
  and best !
  Let me tell you that I love you more than aught on
  earth !"
Then I kissed her o'er and o'er ; and at first she chid
  me sore,*
  But I pled for her forgiveness until she kisséd me ;
Then the time passed like a dream, till the sunset's
  rosy gleam
  Glanced beneath the oak's broad branches on the
  fallen tree.

---

* I suggested " pinched " or " slapped " instead of " chid," but Gubbins obstin-
ately adhered to the original reading.

IV.

Since the raptures of that day, three years had passed
    away,

    When I visited once more the well-remembered spot;

But I traced the path alone, for my faithless girl had
    flown,

    And left me to a desolate and dreary lot.

The fallen tree I found, with the ferny woods around—

    The change was not in them, but in my love and me :

I thought I should have died—but I summoned up
    my pride,*

    And I turned away for ever from the fallen tree.

---

* Here I accused Theopompus of exaggeration in speaking of dying of
a disappointment in love, and suggested that he should alter the line as
follows :—" I thought I should have *cried*"—but the Author indignantly
spurned the amendment, and denied the exaggeration. Should his verses fail
to excite the admiration that he expects, all I can say is, that he cannot lay the
blame on me.

LOYAL PETER.

Air—"Corn Rigs are bonny."

I.

OUR Peter is a writer bauld,
    His style is never muddy, O !
At jobs and quacks he weel can scauld,
    His face is round and ruddy, O !
His shape is portly, middle size,
    He's sturdy in his walkin', O !
The sparklins o' his wit surprise,
    It's fun to hear him talkin', O !
Chorus—Come, Rottenraw and Gallowgate,
        Gusedubs and Briggate smeeky, O !
        And join in praise o' Loyal Pate,
        Wi' Candleriggs sae reeky, O !

. II.

Some quacks sells fusionless pease-meal,
  Pretends it's Revalenta, O !
And brags o' makin' sick folk weel
  In advertisements plenty, O !
A' crammed wi' lees frae en' to en'
  And balderdash sae weary, O !
When Peter he whips out his pen,
  And dings them tapsalteerie, O !
    Come, Rottenraw, &c.

III.

Some knaves, puir simple folk to rob,
  Gets up a scheme ca'd Diddlesex,
But Peter he scents out the job,
  And dings it a' to fiddlesticks.
Our West-End Park will flourish green,
  When summer nights are shorter, O !
Where, but for Peter, would ha'e been
  A park o' bricks and mortar, O !
    Come, Rottenraw, &c.

IV.

Ye rogues o' high and low degree,
　　Scowp aff wi' fear and quakin', O !
If Peter chance your tricks to see,
　　It's then ye'll get a paikin', O !
Ilk honest man and bonny lass,
　　Come, brew the toddy sweeter, O !
And drink wi' me a bumper glass,
　　To the health o' Loyal Peter, O !
　　　　Come, Rottenraw, &c.

THE "SATURDAY REVIEW."

An excellent new Ballad, by a Juvenile Author, to the old tune of
"The Bold Dragoon."

I.

'TWAS some clever little boys, and they grew to smart
  young men,
And they vowed they would amaze the world by
  wielding of the pen ;
So they write a weekly journal, and one reads it now
  and then,—
  'Tis the *Saturday Review*, with its pert, smart, witty
    critics :—
    Whack, fol-de-rol, the pert, smart, witty critics !
    Whack, fol-de-rol, fol-de-riddle, ol-de-ray.

II.

" The *Times* is full of blunders in history and Greek :

And of the other daily prints 'twere waste of time
to speak :

There's neither wit nor sense in those that come out
once-a-week,

Save the *Saturday Review*, with its pert, smart, witty
critics :—

Whack, fol-de-rol, &c.

III.

"Of ancient authors' lumber, and modern authors'
stuff,

There a'nt a dozen volumes that are worth a pinch of
snuff ;

Though stupid writers may combine, each other's works
to puff" :—

Says the *Saturday Review*, with its pert, smart, witty
critics :—

Whack, fol-de-rol, &c.

IV.

" Fred. Schiller lived in Germany, and wrote of Wal-
    lenstein ;
And his tragedy has here and there a passage rather
    fine ;
But the style is far too prosy, and the plot don't
    well combine ;"
  Says the *Saturday Review*, with its pert, smart, witty
    critics :—
        Whack, fol-de-rol, &c.

V.

" And as for Walter Scott, who wrote some forty years
    ago,
He could tell a right good story, and describe a scene
    or so ;
Yet, after all, his tales are but a clever puppet-show ;"
  Says the *Saturday Review*, with its pert, smart, witty
    critics :—
        Whack, fol-de-rol, &c.

VI.

" Some scribblers of the present time, by dint of brag
    and brass,
For poets or philosophers contrive themselves to pass ;
And they suit the British Public, for the Public is
    an ass,"
    Says the *Saturday Review*, with its pert, smart, witty
      critics :—
          Whack, fol-de-rol, &c.

VII.

Now if about the author of this ballad you would know,
At present I'm a little chap, but hope that I shall grow;
And my business is to carry proofs and copy to and fro
    'Twixt the *Saturday Review* and its pert, smart, witty
      critics :—
      Whack, fol-de-rol, the pert, smart, witty critics !
      Whack, fol-de-rol, fol-de-riddle, ol-de-ray.

Διάβολος τυπογραφικὺς.

I.

A LITTLE boy went out one night,
   The little boy went out ;
The moon and stars were very bright
   As he ran round about.

II.

And round, and round, and round about,
   And round about ran he ;
Says he, " I'm running round about,
   Oh round about I be."

III.

His head began to giddy get,
  To giddy get began,
And giddier still, and giddier yet,
  As round about he ran ;

IV.

And then he said unto himself,
  Unto himself, says he,
" Is this myself that's round about,
  And is it really me ? "

V.

And then it grew so very dark,
  So very dark grew it,
That though he often tried to see,
  He could not see a bit.

VI.

And then he thought his eyes were out,
   As out they seemed to be;
Says he, " I think my eyes are out,
   I think they are," says he.

VII.

But his mamma came running out,
   To look for little Sam ;
Says she, " Where are you, Sammikin ? "
   Says Sammy, " Here I am."

VIII.

And when he saw his dear mamma,
   Who Sammy came to find,
He knew by that, as well he might,
   He was not really blind.

D

IX.

And then he knew his eyes were in,
As in they well might be,
Says he, " I think my eyes are in,
" I think they are," says he.

NOTE.—This beautiful poem, in which the most touching simplicity is mingled with the most profound knowledge of the *human heart*, is (as the reader, we are sure, will learn with tears of delight) not altogether a vision of the illustrious author's benign imagination. It is *actually*, as we have been credibly informed, *an almost literal narrative of an incident of the childhood of the famous* DOCTOR SAMUEL JOHNSON (who wrote the big Dictionary and *Rasselas*).

THE HANDSOMEST MAN IN THE ROOM.

Air—" The Charming Woman."

I.

I 'VE always been told that I 'm pretty,
  (And really I think so myself);
I 'm accomplished, good-tempered, and witty,
  And papa has got plenty of pelf.
My teeth, eyes, and curls I won't mention,
  My shape, nor my delicate bloom ;
But I 'm sure I deserve the attention
  Of " the handsomest man in the room,"
Yes, I know I deserve the attention
  Of " the handsomest man in the room."

II.

When I met that sublimest of fellows,
  The sight really made my heart jump;
Other men shrank to mere punchinellos,
  As he towered like a pine in a clump.
So noble and classic each feature,
  With a touching expression of gloom,
That I said to myself—"The dear creature!
  He's the handsomest man in the room!"
"Yes!" I said to myself—"The dear creature!
  "He's the handsomest man in the room!"

III.

He asked me if I'd walk a measure,
  (When he came it was nearly midnight)—
I said—"With a great deal of pleasure,"
  For he danced like a perfect delight.
So in waltzing and polking we sported,
  Till supper sent forth its perfume,

And I went down to table, escorted
  By the handsomest man in the room—
Yes, I went down to table, escorted
  By the handsomest man in the room.

IV.

I thought 'twas a nice situation,
  So snugly together we sat,
And in hopes of a pleasant flirtation
  I tried to engage him in chat.
But, to talk of himself never backward,
  He strove modest airs to assume,
For he told me, he felt very awkward
  As the handsomest man in the room—
" Really, really, one *does* feel *so* awkward
  As the handsomest man in the room ! "

V.

Thought I—" This is really too stupid !
  Your good looks are very well known,

But you ought to know, Grenadier Cupid,
    That I'd much rather hear of *my own.*"
Yet should he reform in this one thing,
    (Of which there are hopes, I presume),
We still may contrive to make something
    Of the handsomest man in the room—
Yes, we still may contrive to make something
    Of the handsomest man in the room.

THE MARRIED MEN'S BALL.

Air—"——'s own favourite galop.'

(Each reader to fill up the blank for himself.)

I.

OF all the right good fellows that the world its surface
    carries on,
The married men of Glasgow are the best beyond
    comparison ;
Resolved of us poor bachelors to earn the lasting
    gratitude,

They've given a ball that fills us all with rapturous
    beatitude.
        Chorus—Whirl about! twirl about! every
            merry girl about!
        Skip about! slip about! like the fairies trip
            about!
        Whisk about! frisk about! nimble as a
            fawn,
        In mirth and joy till morning dawn.

II.

Those married men (I'd readily bet ten to one in fives
    upon't)
Most prudently consulted all their wise and charming
    wives upon't,
And hence the good arrangements, whose completeness
    and diversity
So pleased the new Lord Rector of our ancient Uni-
    versity.
        Whirl about! &c.

III.

The halls are bright with cheerful light and sparkling
    decoration too ;
The shrubs and flowers upon the stair are like a small
    plantation too ;
And lest the flight of time should cause reflections dull
    and vapoury,
The clock face in the gallery is hidden by the drapery.
       Whirl about ! &c.

IV.

The music is so spirited, there's nothing to prevent its
    tone
From rousing into capering a gentleman of twenty
    stone ;
And should he need refreshment, for fatigue there is a
    happy cure—
The supper and the wine would please the most
    fastidious epicure.
       Whirl about ! &c.

V.

Oh ! how it warms one's heart to see the lovely ladies
  glide along,
And swiftly o'er the polished floor in waltz and galop
  slide along,
So beautiful and elegant, so full of grace and suavity,
They'd make a Greek philosopher oblivious of his
  gravity.

Whirl about ! &c.

VI.

Amongst the gentle maidens that adorn this brilliant
  festival,
There's one sweet little darling that I dearly love the
  best of all,
She raises feelings in my breast of such profound
  extensiveness,
That in the midst of all the mirth there comes a touch
  of pensiveness.

Whirl about ! &c.

VII.

Ye bachelors, come join with me in rapturous beatitude,

Expressing to those married men our everlasting grati-
tude ;

Cheer one and all, to shake the hall ; 'twas admirably
done of them ;

But next time that they give a ball, may I myself be
one of them !

Whirl about ! twirl about ! every merry girl
about !

Skip about ! slip about ! like the fairies trip
about !

Whisk about ! frisk about ! nimble as a
fawn,

In mirth and joy till morning dawn !

POSTSCRIPT AND MORAL.

Sure dancing is an antidote to everything that's
horrible,

It clears the brain of care and pain, and bodings dark
and terrible,

And nothing so confounds the machinations of the
  devil as
Those innocent amusements which the fanatics call
  frivolous.
   Skip about ! &c.

ODE

IN PRAISE OF THE CITY OF MULLINGAR.

Air—THE DESERTER—"If sadly thinking."

I.

YE may sthrain your muscles
To brag of Brussels,
  Of London, Paris, or Timbuctoo,
Constantinople,
Or Sebastople,
  Vienna, Naples, or Tongataboo,

Of Copenhagen,
Madrid, Kilbeggan,
  Or the Capital iv the Rooshian Czar;
But they're all infarior
To the vast, suparior,
  And gorgeous city of Mullingar.

II.

That fair metropolis,
So great and populous,
  Adorns the ragions iv sweet Westmeath,
That. fertile county
Which nature's bounty
  Has richly gifted with bog and heath.
Thim scenes so charming,
Where snipes a-swarming
  Attract the sportsman that comes from far;
And whoever wishes
May catch fine fishes
  In deep Lough Owel near Mullingar.

III.

I could stray for ever
By Brusna's river,
  And watch its waters in their sparkling fall,
And the gandhers swimmin'
And lightly skimmin'
  O'er the crystial bosom of the Roy'l Canal ;
Or on Thursdays wander,
'Mid pigs so tender,
  And geese and turkeys on many a car,
Exchangin' pleasantry
With the fine bowld pisantry
  That throng the market at Mullingar.

IV.

Ye nine, inspire me,
And with rapture fire me
  To sing the buildings, both ould and new,
The majestic court-house,
And the spacious workhouse,
  And the church and steeple which adorn the view.

Then there's barracks airy
For the military,
   Where the brave repose from the toils iv war;
Five schools, a nunnery,
And a thrivin' tannery,
   In the gorgeous city of Mullingar.

V.

The railway station
With admiration
   I next must mintion in terms of praise,
Where trains a-rowlin'
And ingynes howlin'
   Strike each behowlder with wild amaze.
And then there's Main Street,
That broad and clane street,
   With its rows of gas-lamps that shine afar;
I could spake a lecture
On the architecture
   Of the gorgeous city of Mullingar.

VI.

The men of genius
Contemporaneous
   Approach spontaneous this favoured spot,
Where good society
And great variety
   Of entertainment is still their lot.
The neighbouring quality
For hospitality
   And conviviality unequalled are ;
And from December
Until November
   There 's still divarsion in Mullingar.

VII.

Now, in conclusion,
I make allusion
   To the beauteous females that here abound ;
Celestial cratures,
With lovely fatures,
   And taper ankles that skim the ground.
E

But this suspinds me,
For the thame transcinds me—
  My muse's powers are too wake by far;
It would take Catullus,
And likewise Tibullus,
  To sing the beauties of Mullingar.

THE STANDARD-BEARER.

(Translated from the German.)

I.

THE Minstrel guards the standard on the plain,
　Upon his arm his trusty sword is lying,
Amidst the stilly night he wakes the strain,
　His harp beneath his blood-stained hand replying :
" The lady that I love I may not name,
　Whose chosen colours on my breast are blending ;
To death I'll fight for freedom and for fame,
　This glorious standard faithfully defending."

II.

The night is o'er; the battle comes with day;
    The minstrel from the standard will not sever;
He waves his sword, and while he sings his lay,
    Each blow strikes down an enemy for ever.
" The lady that I love I may not name,
    Although the foeman's lance my heart were rending,
To death I fight for freedom and for fame,
    This glorious standard faithfully defending."

III.

The fight is won, the deadly strife is past,
    The minstrel on the bloody field is dying,
Beside the standard, faithful to the last,
    His song of love and war still faintly sighing;
" The lady that I love I ne'er shall name,
    My life with joy in honour's cause is ending;
Till death I 've fought for freedom and for fame,
    This glorious standard faithfully defending."

THE CARRICK HILLS.

A new sang to the auld tune of "Major Logan's Compliments
to Miss MacMyn."

I.

COME busk ye braw, my bonnie bride,
And hap ye in my guid gray plaid,
And ower the Brig o' Doon we'll ride
　　Awa' to Carrick Hills, love.

II.

For there's flowery braes in Carrick land,
There's wimplin' burns in Carrick land,
And beauty beams on ilka hand
　　Amang the Carrick Hills, love.

III.

There dwalt my auld forefathers lang,
Their hearts were leal, their arms were strang;
To thee my heart and arm belang
    Amang the Carrick Hills, love.

IV.

I 'll bear thee to our auld gray tower,
And there we 'll busk a blythesome bower,
Where thou shalt bloom, the fairest flower,
    Amang the Carrick Hills, love.

V.

In spring we 'll watch the lammies play,
In summer ted the new-mawn hay,
In hairst we 'll sport the lee-lang day
    Amang the Carrick Hills, love.

VI.

When winter comes wi' frost and snaw,
We'll beet the bleeze and light the ha',
While dance and sang drive care awa'
    Amang the Carrick Hills, love.

1872.

Fables.

F

The Goose and Gridiron.

THE GOOSE AND GRIDIRON.

A GOOSE, proud of her wings, taunted a gridiron with its inability to fly. "Foolish bird!" that utensil replied; "I shall perhaps one day broil those members of which you now boast."

MORAL—*Boast not of transient advantages.*

II.

THE MAGPIE AND STUMP.

A MAGPIE was in the habit of depositing articles which he pilfered in the hollow stump of a tree. " I grieve less," the stump was heard to say, " at the misfortune of losing my branches and leaves, than at the disgrace of being made a receptacle for stolen goods."

MORAL—*Infamy is harder to bear than adverse fortune.*

The Hog in Armour.

III.

THE HOG IN ARMOUR.

A HOG, dreading the usual fate of animals of his species, clothed himself in a suit of armour. "Your precautions," said his owner, "will prolong your life but for a few minutes."

MORAL—*Inevitable evils cannot be averted.*

The Pig and Whistle.

IV.

THE PIG AND WHISTLE.

A COTTAGER, being disturbed by the cries of his pig, tied a whistle on the animal's snout, and thus converted its discord into melody.

MORAL—*True wisdom converts the most unpleasing circumstances into sources of comfort.*

The Cat and Fiddle.

V.

THE CAT AND FIDDLE.

A FIDDLE was boasting of the sweetness of its, voice. "Vain instrument!" exclaimed a cat who stood by, "your notes are but a feeble attempt to imitate mine."

MORAL.—*Art strives in vain to vie with nature.*

VI.

THE GOAT AND COMPASSES.

A PAIR of compasses, belonging to a geographer, was lying on a table, when a goat, happening to pass by, addressed to it the following taunt: "Your limbs serve but to straddle across a piece of paper; mine, to bound over the mountains."

"Your limbs," replied the instrument, "enable one wretched animal to seek its food; mine assist a sage to map the world."

MORAL—*Science, though despised by the ignorant, is better than bodily strength.*

The Belle Savage.

VII.

THE BELLE-SAVAGE.

A BELLE, on some slight provocation, lost her temper, and became savage. "My dear," said her wise aunt, "if you persist in becoming savage, you will soon cease to be regarded as a belle."

MORAL—*Ill-temper is the worst enemy of beauty.*

VIII.

THE CAT AND SALUTATION.

A YOUNG man carried good breeding to a pitch of perfection so exalted, that he would not pass even his grandmother's cat without bowing profoundly by way of salutation.

This conduct so gratified the aged gentlewoman, that she bequeathed to her well-bred grandson the whole of her large fortune, to the exclusion of her other descendants, who were less polite.

MORAL—*Courtesy is due even to the lowliest; and, though costing nothing, is often amply rewarded.*

H

The Swan and two necks.

IX.

THE SWAN WITH TWO NECKS.

A SWAN, being dissatisfied with its single neck and head, implored and obtained from Jupiter the gift of a duplicate provision of those members. The proud bird at first gloried in its acquisition ; but soon its existence was embittered by the frequent struggles and combats of the two necks for articles of food; and, in the end, the swan hailed as a happy release the amputation of one of its necks by the jaws of a voracious pike, which left the other in its primeval condition of peaceful solitude.

MORAL FIRST—*Ambition often suffers by the attainment of its ends.*

MORAL SECOND—*Divided authority is fatal to peace.*

MORAL THIRD—*The loss of superfluous possessions may frequently prove a blessing.*

The Tippling Philosopher.

X.

THE TIPPLING PHILOSOPHER
IN LIQUORPOND STREET.

A PHILOSOPHER, having joined a party of topers in Liquorpond Street, astonished and delighted the company by his wit and joviality, which were at first ascribed to the effect of his frequent potations from a capacious goblet, supposed to contain diluted metropolitan alcohol.* But before the conclusion of the entertainment, the sage invited his companions to taste his beverage, which proved to be pure water; whereupon, with one accord, those previously intemperate individuals renounced, from that time forth, the practice of imbibing ardent spirits.

MORAL FIRST—*The best promoter of gaiety is temperance.*

MORAL SECOND—*Example is better than precept.*

MORAL THIRD—*The true philosopher despises not innocent jocularity.*

* The author is supposed to mean *Gin and Water.—Printer's Devil.*

XI.

THE GREEN MAN AND STILL.

A GREEN man, wandering through the Highlands of Scotland, discovered, in a sequestered valley, a still, with which certain unprincipled individuals were engaged in the illicit manufacture of aqua-vitæ. Being, as we have stated, a green man, he was easily persuaded by those unprincipled individuals to expend a considerable sum in the purchase of the intoxicating produce of their still, and to drink so much of it that he speedily became insensible.

On awaking next morning, with an empty purse and an aching head, he thought, with sorrow and shame, what a green man he had been.

MORAL—*He who follows the advice of unprincipled individuals is a green man indeed.*

XII.

THE BULL AND MOUTH.

A NATIVE of the sister isle having opened his mouth during a convivial entertainment, out flew a bull, whereupon some of the company manifested alarm. "Calm your fears," said the sagacious host; "verbal bulls have no horns."

MORAL—*Harmless blunders are subjects of amusement rather than of consternation.*

WORKS

PUBLISHED BY MR. MACLEHOSE,

PUBLISHER TO THE UNIVERSITY, GLASGOW.

Second Edition, in Extra Fcap. 8vo, Price 6s. 6d., Cloth.

OLRIG GRANGE:

A Poem in Six Books.   Edited by HERMANN KUNST, Philol
Professor.

Examiner.

"This remarkable poem will at once give its anonymous author a high
place among contemporary English poets, and it ought to exercise a potent
and beneficial influence on the political opinions of the cultivated classes.
. . . . The demoralizing influence of our existing aristocratic institutions
on the most gifted and noblest members of the aristocracy, has never been so
subtly and so powerfully delineated as in ' Olrig Grange.'"

Pall Mall Gazette.

"' Olrig Grange,' whether the work of a raw or of a ripe versifier, is plainly
the work of a ripe and not a raw student of life and nature. . . . It has
dramatic power of a quite uncommon class: satirical and humorous obser-
vation of a class still higher; and, finally, a very pure and healthy, if perhaps
a little too scornful, moral atmosphere. . . . The most sickening phase
of our civilization has scarcely been exposed with a surer and quieter point,
even by Thackeray himself, than in this advice of a fashionable and religious
mother to her daughter."

Spectator.

"The story itself is very simple, but it is told in powerful and suggestive
verse. The composition is instinct with quick and passionate feeling, to a
degree that attests the truly poetic nature of the man who produced it. It
exhibits much more of genuine thought, of various knowledge, of regulated
and exquisite sensibility. The author exhibits a fine and firm discrimination
of character, a glowing and abundant fancy, a subtle eye to read the symbol-
ism of nature, and great wealth and mastery of language, and he has employed
it for worthy purposes."

Daily Review.

"A remarkable poem,—a nineteenth century poem,—the work of a genuine
poet, whoever he may be, and of a consummate artist. . . . The story is
wrought out with exquisite beauty of language, and a wealth of imagery
which mark the writer as one full of true poetic sensibility, and keenly alive
to all the subtle influences that are at work in society."

Academy.

"The pious self-pity of the worldly mother, and the despair of the worldly
daughter are really brilliantly put. . . . The story is worked out with
quite uncommon power."

English Independent.

"There is a music in portions of the verse which is all but perfect ; while
for vigorous outline of description, raciness and pungency of phrase, and con-
densation of thought, we know no modern volume of poems that is its equal.
. . . The satire is most searching, the pathos tenderness itself, and once
or twice the passion becomes almost tragic in its intensity. From the first
page to the last the fascination is fully maintained."

Notices of OLRIG GRANGE—*continued.*

Athenæum.

"That it is one of many books which many would do well to read. The monologues are in a metre which is, as far as we know, original, and is eminently well adapted to the semi-ironical tone of this part of the poem. The quaint jolt of the ninth line does the author credit. . . . If the author will rely still further on his own resources, he may produce something as much better than 'Olrig Grange' as that is better than nineteen-twentieths of the poetry we have to read."

Congregationalist.

"There is a pathos and a passion, a depth of sadness and of love, which seems to us to vindicate for this unknown author a very high place among contemporary poets. . . . Most charming is the soliloquy of Hester. . . . The Herr Professor is very much in Hester's thoughts, and the shy surprise, the palpitating wonder, the shame, the pride, the sweet delight, which are all blended in her discovery that she is really falling in love, are perfectly delicious and beautiful . . . but the triumph of the author's genius is in Rose's farewell to her lover."

Tatler in Cambridge.

"One could quote for ever, if a foolscap sheet were inexhaustible ; but I must beg my readers, if they want to have a great deal of amusement, as well as much truth beautifully put, to go and order the book at once. I promise them, they will not repent."

Glasgow Herald.

"We believe that no competent reader will fail to acknowledge the vigour, originality, humour, dramatic power, and imagination which this poem shows."

Scotsman.

"We have said enough to lead our readers, we hope, to take up the book for themselves. It abounds in passages full of suggestion, and contains some of no small poetic beauty, and others of much satirical vivacity and dexterity of expression."

North British Daily Mail.

"It would be easy to cite remarkable instances of thrilling fervour, of glowing delicacy, of scathing and trenchant scorn—to point out the fine and firm discrimination of character which prevails throughout. The lady mother —a proud, grand, luxurious, worldly, mean-minded, canting woman—the author scarifies with a remorseless hate."

Dundee Advertiser.

"If this volume does not place the author in the company of Browning and Tennyson, that is only saying that his book is second to the great masterpieces of contemporary literature."

Liverpool Albion.

"We look upon this poem as an earnest protest against the hollowness and pettiness of much that constitutes society. No moral is obtruded, but the pointed barb of sarcasm is there with its sting, that should act, not indeed as poison, but rather as an antidote."

Echo.

"This is a remarkable poem on contemporary English society, using that term in its most restricted sense, written in a brilliant, humorous, and sarcastic style, but at the same time with a high philosophic aim and a grave moral purpose."

In One Vol., Extra Fcap. 8vo, Cloth, Price 5s.

HILLSIDE RHYMES:

AMONG THE ROCKS HE WENT,
AND STILL LOOKED UP TO SUN AND CLOUD
AND LISTENED TO THE WIND.

Scotsman.

"Let any one who cares for fine reflective poetry read for himself and judge. Besides the solid substance of thought which pervades it, he will find here and there those quick insights, those spontaneous felicities of language which distinguish the man of natural power from the man of mere cultivation. . . . Next to an autumn day among the hills themselves, commend us to poems like these, in which so much of the finer breath and spirit of those pathetic hills is distilled into melody."

Glasgow Herald.

"The author of 'Hillside Rhymes' has lain on the hillsides, and felt the shadows of the clouds drift across his half-shut eyes. He knows the sough of the fir trees, the crooning of the burns, the solitary bleating of the moorland sheep, the quiet of a place where the casual curlew is his only companion, and a startled grouse cock the only creature that can regard him with enmity or suspicion. The silence of moorland nature has worked into his soul, and his verse helps a reader pent within a city to realize the breezy heights, the sunny knolls, the deepening glens, or the slopes aglow with those crackling flames with which the shepherds fire the heather."

Moffat Times.

"The most remarkable thing in these poems is the great and passionate love of nature as displayed on the green hillside, which seems to colour all that the author writes. In this he follows in Wordsworth's footsteps, and seems to have caught the true key-note of his great master. . . . 'Alta Montium : Among the Uplands' constantly reminds us, in its tone and key, of Wordsworth in his highest moods."

Border Advertiser.

"Manor Water in its summer hues, and also when winter mocks the slanting sun, is beautifully described."

North British Daily Mail.

"These 'rhymes,' put before the public in a dress corresponding to the dainty attire in which 'Olrig Grange' was clad, are, for the most part, pure, pleasing, and graceful. . . . They embody certain touching pictures, reminiscences, and reflections; they are instinct with a fine enthusiasm as regards the legendary associations, the pastoral life, and the beautiful scenes of Tweeddale. . . . There is something of Wordsworth in the simple, smooth, flowing lines of 'The Grey Stone on Dollar Law.'"

In One Volume, Extra Fcap. 8vo, Price 5s., Cloth.

THE SONGS AND FABLES OF

the late WILLIAM J. MACQUORN RANKINE, Professor of Civil Engineering in the University of Glasgow, with 10 Illustrations by J. B. (Mrs. Hugh Blackburn).

THE POETICAL WORKS OF
DAVID GRAY.

New and Enlarged Edition. Edited by HENRY GLASSFORD BELL, late Sheriff of Lanarkshire. In One Volume, Extra Fcap. 8vo, price 6s., Cloth.

Scotsman.

"This volume will effectually serve not only to renew, but extend the feeling that the fame and name of David Gray ought not willingly to be let die. His best known poem, 'The Luggie,' abounds in beauties which should be joys for long, if not for ever."

Glasgow Evening Citizen.

"This new and enlarged edition of the poems of David Gray will be hailed by all lovers of genuine poetry. Young as he was, he lived long enough to make his mark. Some of his sonnets are exquisitely fine."

Glasgow Herald.

"It is over twelve years since David Gray, at the age of twenty-three, died at Merkland, Kirkintilloch. It is a misfortune that he was not permitted to live until the season of ripeness; our misfortune, because, judging from the volume before us, we perceive clearly what he might have been, and with what poetic riches he might have dowered the world."

Edinburgh Courant.

"This volume possesses a peculiarity, independent of the gems which it embodies, in that the editing of it was the last literary labour of the late lamented Sheriff of Lanarkshire. The reverential vigour which pervades the equable verse of David Gray is, however, unique; there is a more forcible beauty in his pieces than in those of the Westmoreland poet, and the awe he manifests "for things unseen and eternal" is quite as conspicuous as the deep and steady devotion of the poet of the 'Seasons.' The volume is got up with sufficient taste not to befool the precious things within."

CAMP LIFE

As seen by a Civilian. A Personal Narrative. By GEORGE BUCHANAN, A.M., M.D., Professor of Anatomy in Anderson's University, Glasgow. Crown 8vo, Cloth, 7s. 6d.

Standard.

"This lively and fascinating narrative is the substance of daily jottings in a diary kept by a surgeon in the Crimean war. It certainly comes very late before the public, and must accordingly lose much interest, although it puts on record many things we have not seen elsewhere, or if so, not so well recorded."

Scotsman.

The book contains a variety of readable and interesting sketches, and has about it an air of freshness and originality, partly due, no doubt, to its having been drawn up almost on the spot, and partly also to the pleasant and unaffected style in which the doctor's materials are put together."

THE MAN IN THE MOON,

AND OTHER TALES.

In Imperial 16mo, Cloth gilt, price 3s., Illustrated.

Nonconformist.

"There is a dash, and at the same time a delicacy, about these stories which pleases us. 'The Story of the Little Pond,' and 'The Story of Little Maggie,' have a good deal of originality and whimsical earnestness about them."

Bookseller.

"For a bit of genuine fun, without any pretence to obtruded moral, commend us to the 'Man in the Moon.'"

Spectator.

"The genuine fairy tale has, we much fear, died out with the fairies themselves, and we must be content with such approximations to the true growth as we can find. Even now such a writer as Andersen, or such a story as Ruskin's *Black Brothers*, will bring back the age of gold; but in the main, we should be satisfied if we could always have on hand a supply of stories so simple, pure, and childish in the best sense of the term, as the *Man in the Moon*."

THE PIPITS.

A COMPANION VOLUME TO " CAW ! CAW !"

With Sixteen Page-Illustrations by J. B. (Mrs. Hugh Blackburn.)

In 4to, price 3s.

Courant.

"This is a charming fable in verse, illustrated by the well-known 'J. B.,' whose power in delineating animals, especially birds, is scarcely inferior to Landseer or Rosa Bonheur."

Inverness Courier.

"Even without the aid of the initials, there could be no difficulty in recognizing the illustrations in this charming volume to be by Mrs. Blackburn. They are full of fun, beauty, and character. Mrs. Blackburn seems to pick out instinctively the peculiarities of West Coast birds, and, with a few touches of her pencil, brings up scenes of land and sea-board which may be recognized in a moment."

Glasgow Herald.

"We doubt whether Mrs. Blackburn herself ever drew better birds—more full of expression—more true both to bird nature and the human nature, which her pictures of animals somehow always satirise. . . . The verses are very good—the drawing simply admirable, including, we imagine, bird-portraits of several eminent citizens."

THE SCOTTISH WAR OF INDE-

PENDENCE, its ANTECEDENTS and EFFECTS.
By WILLIAM BURNS. 2 Vols., 8vo, Cloth, 26s.

Scotsman.

"Mr. Burns displays a wonderful amount of research, and a very considerable critical power."

Daily Review.

"Able and learned—the production of an eminent member of the legal profession in Glasgow. . . . His theory is indisputable—that North Britain has from the earliest period been inhabited by an ardent, energetic, high-spirited, *dour* race, who have resolutely and successfully maintained their independence against the incessant attacks of nations mightier and far more numerous than they. . . . The tale of Scotland's wrongs, the patriotic and disinterested ambition of Wallace, the self-seeking of the great nobles, and the high-spirited and generous patriotism of the minor gentry and burghers, have never been so vividly or so acccurately portrayed. . . . Mr. Burns's exposure of the errors and unfounded charges of writers like Mr. Freeman is most complete and withering."

North British Daily Mail.

"We take leave of Mr. Burns with sincere respect for his ability, painstaking research, fairness, and patriotic spirit, which his works display."

WHENCE, AND WHAT IS THE

CHURCH? A Tract for the Times. By a FREE CHURCH LAYMAN. In Crown 8vo, Cloth, 4s. 6d.

Glasgow Herald.

"This excellent book, thoughtful and suggestive, is by a layman and a Free Churchman: but though of the laity, he is quite a match for the clergy, and his Free Churchmanship would liberalize the churches in general, not to say the Free in particular. He is able and accustomed to think, and while he claims and exercises full liberty of thought, he accepts with devout reverence the authority of the written Word of God."

NURSING;

OR, FULL DIRECTIONS FOR THE SICK-ROOM.

By ÆNEAS MUNRO, M.D., 1 Vol., Post 8vo, Cloth, 7s. 6d.

Medical Times and Gazette.

"If more heads of households were familiar with its teaching, it would save them much anxiety and the doctor much unnecessary trouble."

Standard.

"Since Miss Nightingale's book, we have not seen so useful and practical a work on the subject as the work before us."

Just Published, in Extra Fcap. 8vo, Cloth, Price 7s. 6d.

HANNIBAL:

A Historical Drama. By JOHN NICHOL, B. A. Oxon., Professor of English Language and Literature in the University of Glasgow.

Saturday Review.

"After the lapse of many centuries an English poet is found paying to the great Carthaginian the worthiest poetical tribute which has as yet, to our knowledge, been offered to his noble and stainless name."

Athenæum.

"Probably the best and most accurate conception of Hannibal ever given in English. Professor Nichol has done a really valuable work. From first to last of the whole five acts, there is hardly a page that sinks to the level of mediocrity."

Fortnightly Review.

"Upon one figure alone, besides that of his hero, the author has expended all his care and power. Of this one ideal character, the conception is admirable, and worthy of the hand of a great poet. . . . We receive with all welcome this latest accession to the English school of historic drama."

North British Daily Mail.

"'Hannibal,' in all the attributes of dramatic poetry, rises as far above Addison and Dryden as they overtop the paltriness of a modern Vaudeville. . . . But much grander is the final vengeance of Rome upon faithless Capua, and the last banquet of the Campanian chiefs. . . . We do not know what higher praise we can give to the exquisite lyrics which the author has introduced into this scene, than by warning the Laureate that, if Professor Nichol take it into his head to write many more of the same calibre, he must look to his bays."

Glasgow Herald.

"It would be to attribute to Professor Nichol a genius equal to Shakespeare's, or superior even to that, to say that all the difficulties have been triumphantly overcome in the volume before us. But they have been so far surmounted, we venture to say, as to secure for 'Hannibal' a cordial welcome from all who appreciate the historical and classical drama, and to gain for its author a high place among the poets of the present century."

English Independent.

"Had we space, there are many noble passages in the poem we should like to quote. Fulvia's imaginary description of Rome to Hannibal ; the death scene of Archimedes ; and the renewed vows of Hannibal of everlasting enmity to Rome, when his brother's head is brought to him, are particularly worthy of note."

Manchester Guardian.

"Fulvia 'makes a golden tumult in the house,' and carries Roman energy into her love of pleasure, and hatred of the cold and stubborn Roman ways, is perhaps the newest and the most delightful character in Mr. Nichol's play. . . . Mr. Nichol has made the old story live afresh. . . . Mr. Nichol is certain to please his readers ; but the audience of historical drama, however fit, is a scanty one, and what the poet has to say deserves the widest hearing.

Notices of HANNIBAL—*continued.*

Manchester Examiner.
"We know no modern work in which the dignity of history has been so justly regarded by a poet possessed of such intense admiration for his hero."

Echo.
"Professor Nichol has produced a scholarly and polished work."

Dublin Telegraph.
"Professor Nichol has just given us a volume which bids fair to open a new era in poetry, and secures to the author a position among the first poets of the day."

Morning Post.
"Glasgow has good reason to be proud of her Professor of English Literature, in which he now takes a prominent place by right of his admirable classic drama. Criticism will award him a regal seat on Parnassus, and laurel leaves without stint."

Scotsman.
"But there is much more than mere historical power in 'Hannibal.' Mr. Nichol seems to us to possess real dramatic genius. His personages are not merely types of Carthaginian or Roman, but they are real men and women. They are nearly all conceived under the influence of a generous sympathy with the strong and heroic qualities of character. . . . As regards dramatic power, and the spirited representations of action, we think it no disparagement to them (Arnold and Swinburne) to say that we prefer 'Hannibal' either to 'Merope' or to 'Atlanta in Calydon.'"

Westminster Review.
"Professor Nichol has thrown his fine poem 'Hannibal' into a dramatic form, simply because his whole tone is dramatic. He throws himself into each of his characters. . . . In Myra's speeches we have the ring of antique valour. . . . The beauties of the lyrics, which are scattered with so lavish a hand throughout the volume, resemble the odes in a Greek play, rather than the songs of our own dramatists. . . . 'Hannibal' is a remarkable poem, it stands out alone, by itself, from all other modern poems."

A SYSTEM OF MIDWIFERY;
including the Diseases of Pregnancy and the Puerperal State. By WILLIAM LEISHMAN, M.D., Regius Professor of Midwifery in the University of Glasgow. In One Thick Vol., 8vo (860 Pages and 183 Wood Engravings), Price 30s.

Practitioner.
"In many respects, not only the best treatise on midwifery that we have seen, but one of the best treatises on any medical subject that has been published of late years."

Lancet.
"We have little hesitation in saying that it is, in our judgment, the best English book on the subject."

British and Foreign Medical Chirurgical Review.
"We can recommend this work as unquestionably the best modern book on midwifery in our language."

www.ingramcontent.com/pod-product-compliance
Lightning Source LLC
Chambersburg PA
CBHW020406030726
47496CB00007B/2335